This book is dedicated to those
who stay curious and encourage
the curiosity in others.

In an everyday town
on an everyday street

Lived a curious girl I do
wish you could meet

She was up every morning
with her nose in a book

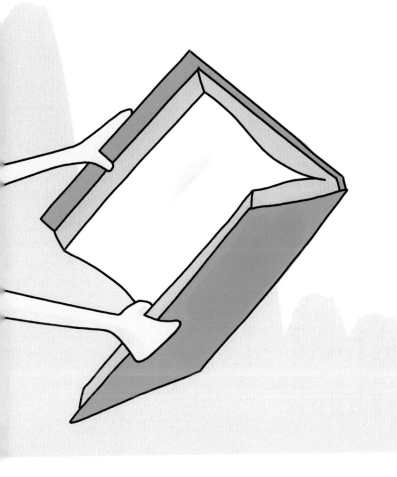

"There is so much to learn!
Come and see! Take a look!"

From waking to sleeping
she would wonder aloud

"Can a bumblebee talk?"
"What holds up a cloud?"

"What makes flowers grow?"
"How do hummingbirds fly?"

"Do earthworms have eyes?"
"Why do onions make me cry?"

Not afraid of the thought of what something might be

She'd ask "what did you find there? Oh please move! Let me see!"

She was ever so curious
of noises at night

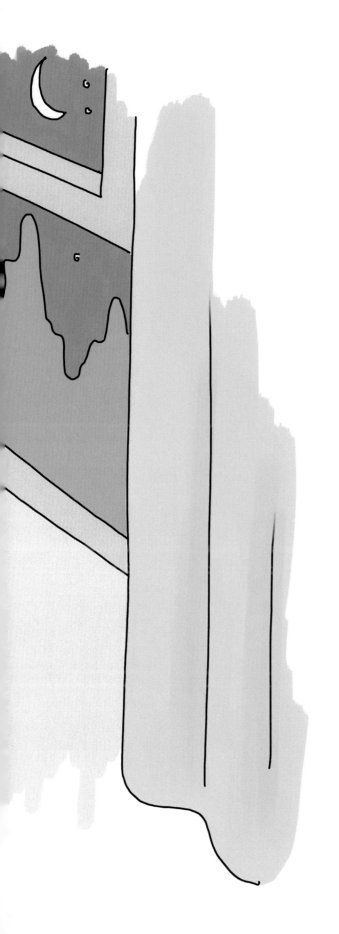

"I want to hear more, Mom! Please turn off the light!"

When her brother said
creatures lived under her bed

She excitedly made traps
with boxes and thread.

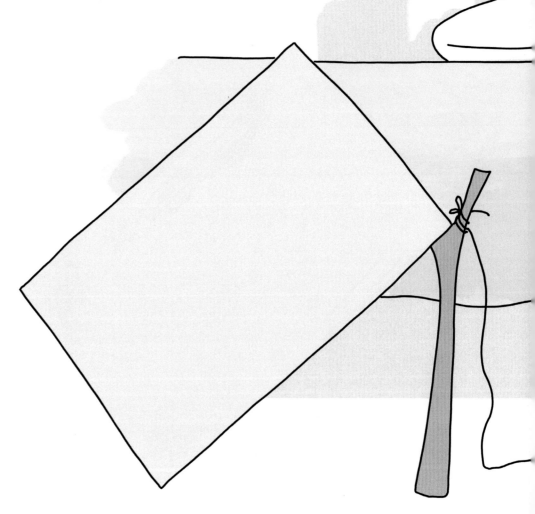

When classmates
refused to eat food
that was new

She'd say "Purple
striped broccoli!
May I have a few?"

But to be an explorer means sometimes you might

Get hurt, tired or angry when things don't go right.

While mapping the moon with her paper and pen

She was bitten by hungry mosquitos and then

She found catching
tadpoles by hand is
not fun

When you slip in
the mud and don't
even catch one.

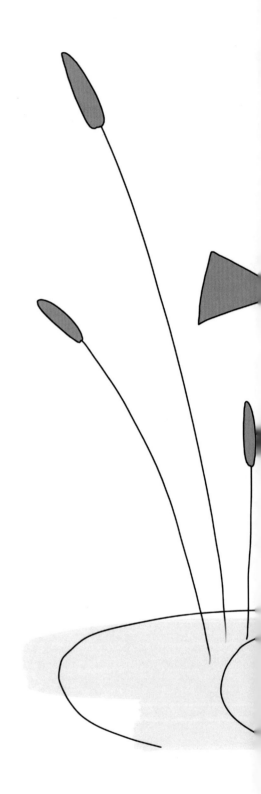

But fail or succeed she
would always take note

So that others could learn
from the things that she wrote

Mosquito spray lets you draw
outside without scratching

And nets with long handles
are better for catching

As she grew older
she never stopped
yearning

For knowledge,
adventure, new
places and learning

She found wonderful
things in search of
what's true

High mountains, deep
oceans explored as
she grew

So tonight in the
sky, you might see
a bright dot

Moving fast like
a comet

(I assure you it's not)

It's a ship above Earth
watching galaxies swirl...

With a crew and
brave captain

A most
curious girl.

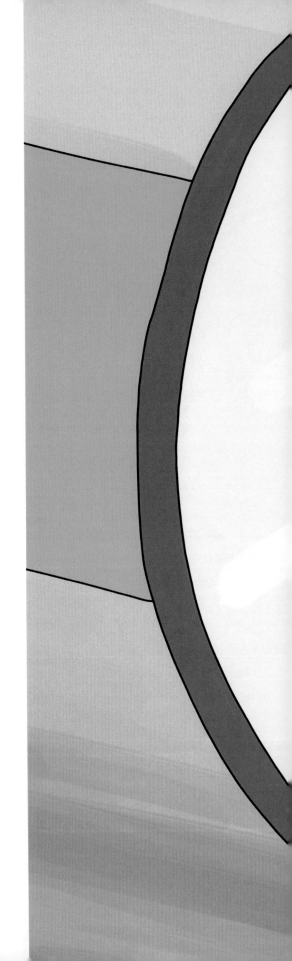

NO WAY!

We are just
getting started...

Notes on how to

STEP 1: Ask a question based on an observation.

STEP 2: Make a prediction (sort of like a thoughtful guess) that you can test.

STEP 3: EXPERIMENT!

TEST THE IDEA

my fav!

STEP 4: Hmm... Observe and measure what happened. (Don't forget to write it down!)

STEP 5: Draw conclusions. What do the results suggest? What did we learn or discover?

STEP 6: SHARE WHAT YOU FOUND!

You can't keep a great discovery to yourself :)

My Curious Discoveries

_____

_____

_____

_____

_____

_____

_____

_____

_____

_____

_____

_____

Made in the USA
Middletown, DE
19 December 2018